T0148585

Life Marrow

A True Story of a Family

DESTIN WRITER

BALBOA.PRESS

A DIVISION OF HAY HOUSE

Balboa Press books may be ordered through booksellers or by contacting:

Balboa Press
A Division of Hay House
1663 Liberty Drive
Bloomington, IN 47403
www.balboapress.com.au
1 (877) 407-4847

Because of the dynamic nature of the Internet, any web addresses or links contained in this book may have changed since publication and may no longer be valid. The views expressed in this work are solely those of the author and do not necessarily reflect the views of the publisher, and the publisher hereby disclaims any responsibility for them.

The author of this book does not dispense medical advice or prescribe the use of any technique as a form of treatment for physical, emotional, or medical problems without the advice of a physician, either directly or indirectly. The intent of the author is only to offer information of a general nature to help you in your quest for emotional and spiritual well-being. In the event you use any of the information in this book for yourself, which is your constitutional right, the author and the publisher assume no responsibility for your actions.

Any people depicted in stock imagery provided by Getty Images are models, and such images are being used for illustrative purposes only. Certain stock imagery © Getty Images.

Print information available on the last page.

ISBN: 978-1-5043-2168-6 (sc)
ISBN: 978-1-5043-2169-3 (e)

Balboa Press rev. date: 07/15/2020

FOREWORD

'Life Marrow' is a deeply personal memoir about love, loss, and family, driven by a quiet strength and introspection.

What a beautifully told sharing of a difficult journey. The yearning and self-reflection and the striving for hope that characterise the narration will draw readers in. The sweetness of a father's devotion to and joy with his son will warm hearts. Readers will appreciate the candour and willingness to share.

AUTHOR'S NOTE

'Life Marrow' came into being during the toughest time of my life when I started relieving excruciating emotional pain through writing. I had written over fifty pages when the idea of turning it into a book crossed my mind. And I made it happen.

Writing this memoir was not easy and involved lots of tears, but opened my heart to live with gratitude and feel the joy of life.

Destin Writer
destinwriter@gmail.com

PREFACE

'Life Marrow' is a true story of a family, whose beloved two-year-young son was diagnosed with leukaemia in February 2017. People and places are real, and events and dates are precise. All the names are pseudonyms. The story reflects on the feelings, emotions, and challenges the author has faced as a father and family man during tragic events.

This book was born on a squeaky bed of the oncology ward of the children's hospital in Sydney, Australia, when a father's heart was aching from what his son was going through. This remarkable diary is a powerful reminder of love, parenthood, resilience, vulnerability, and family relationships.

To my loving son, whose patience, resilience, and understanding have inspired me.

CONTENTS

Foreword v

Author's Note vi

Preface... vii

Chapter 1   Early 2017 1

Chapter 2   Shocking News 11

Chapter 3   First Few Days 17

Chapter 4   New Job 38

Chapter 5   Next Three Months............................. 48

Chapter 6   My Marriage 61

Chapter 7   End of Treatment 83

Chapter 8   Daddy's Place 91

Chapter 9   Christmas 105

CHAPTER 1

Early 2017

It was the beginning of 2017 in Sydney, Australia. I had enjoyed a delightful Christmas and New Year with family and friends, in particular with my wonderful two-year-young son, Lucas. I started the New Year with lots of hope to advance my career, improve my financial position, and spend time with my son.

I often played guitar for Lucas, and he sang along with me in his own sweet language. He was so funny when singing, but he sounded in tune. It seemed he had a good ear for music. He was a happy and cheeky boy who made me laugh. I felt I wanted to dedicate my life to him. His love fulfilled me. Everything at home was about him. I could not wait to return from work to be with my son, play with him, and put him to sleep. Many nights I took him to bed, gave him lots of kisses and cuddles, read a story for him, and sang a song until he was fast asleep in my arms. I had recorded his beautiful voice when he sang along with me.

I saw myself in Lucas. I felt I looked at my younger self and experienced my beautiful childhood moments through my son. It was a strange feeling.

I have lovely memories of my childhood in a warm family. Most evenings, we all watched television or a movie together, while the tantalising smell of my mum's bubbling stew wafted into the living room from the kitchen. My dad often worked on his architecture sketches while watching television with us. After dinner, we went to sleep early, at around nine o'clock. Sometimes, my brother and I took our little sister with us in an adventure to find out what Mum and Dad watched after they sent us to our beds. One night, my dad caught us at the crime scene, where we boys cheekily ran away, and our poor little sister took the blame—an unforgettable funny story we laughed over for many years.

We often had family gatherings and parties at our house. We were filled with laughter, games, dance, and music. We played guitar and sang lovely songs for hours. My dad had a voice, and almost every night I heard his warm voice singing beautiful songs. We loved music, rehearsed singing, and recorded our voices. Our home was full of life and the sound of love. The family was the marrow of our lives, to which my parents dedicated themselves.

My father loved his family and was proud of himself as a family man. He stressed a lot about the value of the family and taught us to care about our family more than everything else.

Everything was beautiful until my father went bankrupt while I was studying the second year of engineering at university. My mother left a year later, took my sister with her, and lived with my grandma for a few years.

I was at university with my roommates when I received a call from my brother to tell me that Mum and Dad had gotten divorced. It was sudden and shocking news. But for years, I did not share the story with any of my friends. My university friends said I was not fun to hang out with any longer and asked what was wrong, but I did not open up. I wish I had.

I think subconsciously I did not want my social status to fall because I felt shame about the divorce. I felt I was from a failed family. My dad had taught me the value of family, but that value was gone. I was afraid to expose my vulnerability and shame, so I kept it all inside. I wish I'd had the courage to share my feelings, rather than carrying all that pressure alone.

My dad, my brother, and I rented a tiny apartment and lived in that fashion for a few years. Watching my dad drown in debt and fight to keep his feet on the ground was hurtful. All the laughter and happiness of my youth turned into a distant dream. My heart ached for our lovely family, who'd fallen apart in a blink of an eye.

My dad got depression and lost his dignity and respect as the man of our family. He never recovered. He worked so hard to keep us together and never gave up on his family.

When I was in my late twenties, our financial position improved. My mother returned, and we created our family again, but with lots of scars in our relationships.

In my early twenties, I avoided my friends and broke up with my girlfriend because I felt embarrassed about my family, unlike before, when I had felt proud of them. It was an excruciating feeling of shame, which I ignored. I had lost my self-confidence, but I did not show it.

I still remember a beautiful girl in university who liked me. I liked her too, but I pushed her away and did not show my real feelings for her. I watched someone else be with her, which was painful. But I had dulled my emotional pain. I went into myself for years and became a tense and lonely bloke, disconnected from everyone. I numbed my feelings and desire for girls because it seemed too distant to achieve, and it was easier to forget than to face my problems.

My only friend was my guitar. I had no girlfriend for all those best years of my youth—until the age of twenty-eight, when I started to find friends. And soon I met Emily.

In 2017, Emily and I had been together for fourteen years, married for twelve. In the eyes of others, we were a great match. She was an artist and had displayed her artwork in a few Sydney galleries. I felt proud of her. I had hung many of her paintings on the walls of our place. Emily had also worked in fashion design. She made her bespoke, elegant dresses herself, and many made-to-measure shirts and jackets for me.

I always felt her love for me when she took my measurements. Sometimes, I was playful and did not let her finish, and we ended up in bed! We often had great sex, and we both enjoyed it.

We often watched movies while she was in my arms. Emily liked heated discussions over our favourite champions when we watched the Australian Open. Even if we both were fans of the same player in a match, she picked the opposite one to make watching the game enticing. We both enjoyed outdoors and used to lace up our hiking shoes and paddle in stunning bays around Sydney.

Emily loved the smoke of my barbecue on weekends and always complimented me on its exquisite recipe. We sometimes made bread together, and I kneaded the dough.

We often invited our friends over to our place and held parties. Emily enjoyed making lots of delicious food, sweets, and cakes, and I was responsible for making barbecue and washing the dishes.

Our life was about love, family, and friendship. Emily and I were soul mates.

I had been struggling to buy a house in Sydney, chasing the property prices, which had doubled in a few years. Buying a house had always been a priority, and it became even more important after my son was born.

The birth of my son was the best experience of my life. When I met Lucas for the first time, he stole my heart and never returned it to me. He bound my soul by his lovely smile and sweet voice when he started to say, 'Daddy.' And the bind grew even stronger when he said, 'Hey, Dad.'

As a father, I wanted the best for him. But I was disturbed by constant worries about the future. I always wanted a large backyard to build a wooden tree house for my son. I enjoyed making wooden things. I had built our coffee table, television unit, and a unique oil colour case for Emily. I had made the oil colour case with love only for her, as she wanted it.

I felt I had let Emily down, since I could not provide financial stability for her. We bought an apartment at the start of our marriage. In 2010, I left it for my parents to have peace of mind, rather than renting at their age. Emily did not object, as she loved them like her parents. She never mentioned it, but I felt she was just considerate. She had undoubtedly thought, if we had sold it, we would have been well ahead. I always felt embarrassed about it because of my broken family.

Although I had a well-paid professional career, I was feeling helpless and desperate to buy a house. In my head, I sometimes blamed Emily because, if she had worked even part-time in the past many years, we would have had enough cash to sort it out. We could have enjoyed raising our little boy in our family house, rather than worrying about house prices. Owning a house had become a big deal in my head. The worrying was killing me and was affecting my behaviour. It was mainly my responsibility to build our family home. I had to do something, but I was not sure what. I was insecure about the future of my family. It brought back the memories of my dad's drowning ship, and I did not want the same for my family.

In mid-January 2017, I received a call from a recruitment agency about a role on a project in the

New South Wales government. I would work with a team I had worked with before, but with higher pay and a senior role. It looked like an excellent opportunity.

I was frustrated about the level of my engagement in my current job, and I was uncertain about my career growth. Besides, it would take years for me to reach the income the new job offered.

I approached my manager, Nathan, the new finance director, and expressed my honest feelings. I asked if there was a prospect for career progression. He did not give me a hopeful outlook. My colleagues encouraged me to take the opportunity.

I pursued the role, and after two interviews, I got the job! I felt positive and successful.

'This job should provide us with extra savings, which we can put aside for buying a house,' I said to Emily with hope.

I was supposed to start my new job on Monday, 27 February 2017. It was a few weeks away. I was handing over the work to my colleagues and getting ready for departure.

I wrote my resignation letter in an email, but something was stopping me from submitting it. I always trust what my heart says. Therefore, I thought to review and send my email a day after. I tried day after day but could not submit it. I had changed jobs as a consultant many times. It was an unusual nervousness. I talked to Nathan and Laura, the HR director; expressed my concerns; and requested to use my three weeks remaining leave instead of resigning. Both Nathan and Laura accepted my request. I could return if my new job did not work out well. I was grateful and felt valued.

I hope everything will be fine.

CHAPTER 2

Shocking News

On Thursday, 23 February, a beautiful and sunny day, I finished lunch and was walking back to the office thinking about the start of my new role in four days.

My phone rang. It was Emily.

'Lucas,' said Emily, weeping and unable to continue.

I tried to calm her down.

'What's wrong? Is Lucas okay?' I asked.

'Lucas has leukaemia—blood cancer,' said Emily.

I shivered and felt cold. My heart was pounding. I stopped walking and asked for more information.

'A paediatrician saw Lucas, and from the initial symptoms, diagnosed him with leukaemia. The doctor took a blood test to confirm. He advised me to prepare for a few days stay in the children's hospital. He will call before four o'clock to let me know,' said Emily.

'I hope the test result is negative, but I'm coming home now,' I told Emily.

This *hope* is what one would need to deal with severe situations, I believe.

Lucas had been unwell for a few weeks, which looked like flu. Three general practitioners examined him and told us there was nothing serious other than a virus—until Emily insisted on seeing a specialist. A paediatrician who had worked in the oncology centre for many years saw him and immediately diagnosed him with leukaemia.

Mum's instinct alarmed her, I believe. She told me a day before the diagnosis, 'I think something is wrong with Lucas. I know!'

However, I thought it would be the mum's thing of being worried all the time.

'We just saw a doctor. Don't worry. He is fine,' I told her.

But I was wrong. Her feelings were correct.

I ran to the office; grabbed my bag; and rushed out of the office, heading home. My workmates were at lunch.

On my way out, I saw Liz, a colleague of mine.

'You look pale. Are you all right?' said Liz as soon as she saw me.

'My son Lucas is not okay. It might be leukaemia,' I reluctantly replied, while looking away.

'Huh … Go … Go quickly, hope everything is okay,' said Liz.

I never forgot that *huh* and her initial reaction, a natural response to a traumatic situation. And *hope everything is okay* was the same hope we all need to ease things. Her reply made me emotional and brought tears to my eyes.

Thank God I have travelled to work by train today! It is safer, I thought to myself, since I usually drove to work.

I went to the train station. The train arrived in a few minutes, but it felt a lifetime. Once I sat on the train, a million thoughts ran through my head about Lucas. I looked at his pictures on my mobile phone, which brought tears to my eyes. I could not see things clearly or hear anything other than noises in my head. I do not remember if people looked at me or said anything to me. From the time I was on the train until I held my son in my arms was one of the most daunting moments of my life. But it was not the most daunting. That was still to come!

I got home. Before I entered, I pulled myself together to support my wife.

For God's sake, stop shivering. Men are supposed to be strong! I said to myself.

I entered our home and hugged Emily. She wept hard. She had told no one other than a friend of hers, who was a doctor. My son was asleep. We looked at his pale face for a while, with tears rolling down our cheeks. We felt we were losing him. It is a natural human behaviour that the worst comes to mind, but then you fight for life with hope.

Emily had already packed her bag for an overnight stay in the hospital. We focused and thought about our needs to manage the situation. I could not wait for the call from the paediatrician. I called his mobile, which he had given to Emily. The paediatrician suggested that I contact the laboratory and follow up for returning the test result before the end of the working hours. I rushed to the laboratory in person. They advised the sample had gone to the central laboratory, and we had to wait.

At around four o'clock, the paediatrician called me. I leapt to my feet to answer the phone. Emily was standing in front of me, staring at me with distressed eyes.

'I received the test result, which confirms the diagnosis of leukaemia. Sorry for the news. I know you may be in shock, but it is treatable. You need to go to the children's hospital now. They will look after your son. I have contacted them and arranged everything,' said the paediatrician.

'Okay, we'll go now,' I said with a shaky voice.

Tears came to my eyes. The news broke my back. I later realised that subconsciously, I still had hoped for a negative test result, knowing the chance was small. It reminded me of the means of *hope* in life. I got over my emotions and focused on supporting my son and my wife.

We jumped in the car and went to the children's hospital, not knowing what was ahead of us. It was peak hour, and traffic was heavy on Sydney roads. We were both nervous, and Emily was crying. I was driving with one hand on the steering wheel and one hand taking Emily's hand. I regularly checked on Lucas through the mirror. He had sensed the problem and looked anxious. I could not tell if he was in pain. He was not crying, but he might have been too weak to complain. My head was spinning with various thoughts while I was driving.

I hope everything will be fine.

✦

CHAPTER 3

First Few Days

We arrived at the hospital emergency. They were expecting us. After the initial checks, a doctor saw Lucas and advised his blood count was low. He needed a blood transfusion for red cells and platelets.

'We will do a series of tests to determine the cancer type and establish a treatment plan,' said the doctor.

I was all ears and ready to memorise the jargon. I searched for new terminologies on the internet to learn and prepare myself. I chronicled the medical procedures and test results every day.

Emily's friend and her husband visited us in the hospital emergency and brought a pizza for us. She provided emotional support to Emily.

My little son was flat. He only asked for milk with a weak voice. The experience was daunting and scary. I felt nervous and tried not to think about it much. Otherwise, I would get overemotional. Right or wrong, I did not openly display my inner pain as a man to support my family. After all, my options were limited, and I had to go with life wherever it would take me.

We stayed at the hospital emergency for a few hours. They then transferred us to a ward with seven beds, with kids of varied ages and diseases on each bed. A nurse came around and told us an oncology specialist doctor would soon visit us.

It was nerve-racking and exhausting enough to be hospitalised, and many disruptive noises at night were annoying. The alert sound of the infusion pump and the three beeps of the nurse call button every few minutes got on my nerves. Lucas had to be fasting from midnight until the next morning because of his operation under general anaesthetic.

Seeing Lucas in pain brought back my childhood memories—my beautiful parents and their love, care, and hard work for me. Although I had never stayed a night in a hospital before, thank God, I'd had a gastric ulcer for ten years from the age of nine. I always had an annoying stomach ache all those years. My dad was persistent in taking me to the best specialists to relieve me from pain. My dad loved me, and I loved him too. I knew how Lucas felt when I was there for him—the same feeling of love and support I had felt from my dad.

The next morning on 24 February, a nurse came to the ward and asked us to go with her to a private room for a consultation session. It brought a sinking feeling to my stomach. Emily and I were both nervous. It felt like bad news, which they did not want to say in front of others. But the privacy was in fact for us to be comfortable, without feeling that others were watching us. It was the most stressful and daunting moment of my life. My whole body was tense and shaky, and sometimes I put my hand on my leg to stop it from shivering.

A team was in the room waiting for us. The nurse introduced Sharon, the oncology specialist doctor, and John, the social worker. They explained what leukaemia was and what would be ahead of Lucas. It was an informative and helpful session but nerve-racking.

'The treatment will take about two years, with intense chemotherapy of about six months. The type and intensity of treatment depend on the result of the tests we will do today,' said Sharon.

Sharon explained they would insert a tube called a central line into the large vein through Lucas's chest. They used this tube to take blood samples and to give him medications, rather than needling him many times a day. The tube would be attached to him for a few months during the intense treatment period.

Thinking my son's two years of life would be chemotherapy in the hospital broke my heart. I had many plans in my head to take my son to the beach and play with him. All that joy seemed so distant, like a dream.

During the meeting, I realised that Emily felt devastated much more than I had foreseen. She had lost her dad because of leukaemia, and now her son had been diagnosed with the same disease. It would be too hard for her.

After the session, I went out of the meeting room while Emily was still there and explained my worries about Emily to John, who was a kind and helpful man.

He advised they would take any opportunity to explain to Emily that there was no proof that leukaemia was genetic, so she would not feel she had caused pain for her son.

After the session, we went back to the ward to prepare for three operations—lumbar puncture, a bone marrow test, and inserting the central line under general anaesthetic.

My close friend Sam who lived in Brisbane called me. I went out of the ward and told him what had happened to Lucas. I had a shaky voice and twitching lips. The distressful news shocked him. He did not know what to say. We always talked on the phone, but that conversation sounded weird because it was unexpected for him.

While I was talking on the phone, I saw the anaesthetic specialist entered the ward to explain the procedure before the operation. I ended the call and went back to the ward.

Sam called me later on in the day, sympathised with me, and said his wife had shed a lake of tears after hearing the news. We had been close friends for twenty years. They had travelled from Brisbane to Sydney for Lucas's first birthday party.

After the anaesthetic specialist explained the procedure, they transferred Lucas to the operating room. Only one parent could stay with him until they put him to sleep. Emily wanted to go with Lucas. It was hard to see my little boy going under a surgical operation, but we did not have a choice.

For every operation, I had to sign a few pages of paperwork written in a tiny font. I thought it was unnecessary. Parents in such a distressful situation cannot read all the information. It was to protect the hospital's rights in case of any issues.

We had to wait in the parents' room for about three hours, which allowed me to accept the fact that my son was under his first of many operations, and I had to stay positive and support him in his tough journey. Emily and I talked about this, and we both agreed that the most crucial feeling our son needed from us was assurance. Children are smart in understanding what their parents feel. We both pledged ourselves to switch our mindset from a traumatic state to a more positive state and be playful with him at all times.

After the operation, the nurses let us into the recovery room to see Lucas. His face was puffy. He asked for milk with a rough and scratchy voice because of the side effects of the anaesthetic. We could not give him milk, and instead, we offered him apple juice. He drank the apple juice with an appetite, which gave me a strong sense of hope.

He can do it; he will be all right, voices in my head said to me.

The first thing that drew my attention was his central line on his chest. The central line was a tube inserted into the chest through the skin into the large vein to give him chemotherapy drugs and take blood without needling him all the time. For the whole period of intense treatment, about six to eight months, the tube would dangle from his chest. Looking at his central line brought tears to my eyes, but thinking he would feel less pain than being needled multiple times a day took the tears away.

With his rough voice, he asked me to play his favourite song, to which he always danced. I chuckled; he was so funny. Just after an operation, he wanted to dance! I felt he was a tough boy. He was the one giving us hope and strength. It seems odd, but it is true. I looked around at other parents. We were all on the same boat, with similar experiences and emotions.

After recovery, we went back to the ward. Lucas was well conscious and alert. Emily's aunt, Julie; her uncle, Edward; and Lucas's eleven-year-young cousin, Martin, came to the hospital to visit Lucas. Julie brought lots of food for us, which was nice. Their presence made us feel much better. Lucas loved Martin, and his company made him happy. He asked for his favourite songs, and Martin played them for him on the monitor each bed had. Lucas shook his body with a cheeky smile to his favourite songs, though he was stuck on a bed receiving fluids and the medication. Even just after an operation, he remained cheerful and made everyone laugh.

Some of our friends came to the hospital to see Lucas, and all tried to help. But I realised it was a difficult situation to be helpful. On the one hand, we wanted peace to deal with our emotions; on the other hand, we needed support. I met some families who allowed no visitors except their immediate family members.

Some visitors brought food, which was helpful. Some did not know what to say or do and stayed quiet, which I found unpleasant. Four of our friends visited Lucas in the hospital. He was on his bed receiving fluids; they were with Lucas and me in the room, and Emily was out of the room talking to a friend of hers. They were not saying even one word and not playing with Lucas to cheer him up. They were standing and staring at him as if they had come to a funeral.

Lucas felt uncomfortable and asked me for a cuddle. He was in my arms, and I was feeling terrible inside. I did not know what to say. I appreciated their visit, but they were disturbing us. I felt my chest was tightening. My lips felt a twitch, and tears rolled down my cheeks while Lucas was in my arms. I could not control myself.

It was not their fault at all. They did not understand the situation and did not know how to empathise with us. Even after I shed tears, none of them touched my shoulder to sympathise with me. They watched us without saying a word and, after a few minutes, left!

It also upset me that some relatives wanted to take a photo with Lucas while his face was not looking healthy and he was not feeling well. We had to ask them not to take any pictures.

My colleagues sent me many kind messages that their thoughts were with my family, and they prayed for my son in their daily prayers. I felt I was not alone and knew the thoughts of the surrounding people were with my family.

It is important to sympathise with others when they are in need, but it is also essential to know how to empathise. In sympathising with others, ignoring the situation and giving false hope will not help. Saying things like, 'Don't worry; it's nothing; he will be fine,' is dumb. One cannot say, 'It's nothing,' because it is something serious. And to say, 'Do not worry,' is an unreasonable expectation. Some people do not understand the emotions parents go through when their child has a severe illness.

Instead, listening well and understanding parents' needs will help ease their pain. Say things like, 'My thoughts are with you and your son,' or, 'I wish you strength,' or, 'I understand, it's hard,' or, 'I wish all goes well with the operation,' or simply ask, 'How are you feeling?'. You acknowledge the situation and wish families what they need—like strength and recovery.

Nurses and social workers were so helpful. They knew what to say and how to keep us informed. Their smiles were priceless. I was grateful to them. They are special people with big hearts. They often see suffering and loss of children and their heartbroken parents, but they can absorb it all and keep up their smiles and hard work. What a rewarding job they have!

Different nurses saw us and repeated the same information because they knew we were in shock, and we would not absorb all the information at once, which gave us a chance to ask questions as they came to mind.

They gave Lucas a few rounds of red blood cells and platelets, which helped him to feel much better. They also gave him antibiotics to reduce the risk of infection because his immune system was down. Infection was the most critical risk factor. A nurse came around and gave us a thermometer to monitor Lucas's temperature.

Nurses were watching his condition, which was assuring. I felt my son was in good hands, and they were on top of the situation. Looking around, I saw many children in need of blood transfusion. I had donated blood about once or twice a year, but I better understood how crucial blood donation is. I pledged myself to donate blood at least four times a year as long as I would be healthy. Giving blood is the minimum I can contribute to the health of others.

After Lucas's condition was stable and under control, I reminded myself that I was starting a new job on Monday. John was around, and I thought I'd consult with him about changing my job. Being in a state of shock, I was worried to make a wrong decision. I had enough on my plate and did not want to complicate my knotty life further.

John advised me that the journey ahead would be tough and would demand a lot of time in the hospital from us. He said we should consider the hospital our second home for a while. He was also accommodating in providing letters to both organisations explaining my situation, so they would better understand what was involved, which would make my conversations with them easier.

'I am supposed to start on Monday, but I am not sure if I can. We are at the children's hospital and just found out that my son has leukaemia. I am in shock and don't know what to expect. More tests will determine the treatment plan. As soon as I get more information, I'll discuss this with you.' I sent a text message to Jennifer, my direct manager of the new contract, with whom I had worked previously.

'This is shocking and distressing news. I'm so sorry for your family. Please don't worry about work. We can talk next week when you have more information. If I can do anything, please let me know,' replied Jennifer.

On Saturday, 25 February, Sharon saw us and explained they had the test results, and the type of leukaemia was Pre-B ALL. She was a positive and helpful doctor with a lovely smile and an Irish accent that sometimes I struggled to understand. But over time, I got used to her accent. Sharon said the cure rate for Lucas's diagnosis was high. As soon as she said that, tears came to my eyes but cheery tears. *Hope* flourished again in me.

She explained the medications for Lucas and their side effects. The steroid was one of the main ones, which would make Lucas moody and irritable and increase his appetite. He would temporarily get chubby because of the steroid.

'After giving Lucas the initial dose of chemotherapy, the tests so far have shown good progress. Paul, the senior specialist doctor, will also come and talk to you tomorrow with more details of the treatment plan,' said Sharon.

On 26 February, Paul saw Lucas. He talked with confidence, and I could trust him. He was transparent and explained everything. I liked his approach. Paul did not give us false hope but genuine hope.

'Although leukaemia is a rare disease in children, the type Pre-B ALL is a common type of cancer in children. The cure rate is high for this cancer, but there are risks involved. There are a few bone marrow tests on days eight, fifteen, thirty-three, and seventy, which collectively define the risk level for Lucas. The risk level will determine the treatment plan and the intensity of chemotherapy—which will affect the short- and long-term side effects. The first phase of treatment is the same for everybody, regardless of the risk level. If the risk level is high, the chemotherapy would need to be stronger for the following phases, and he would need a bone marrow transplant. The treatment takes about two years, with lots of visits and overnight stays in the hospital for six months and then tablets at home for eighteen months. If there is any complication, this might change, but most children do well,' said Paul.

'The first phase of treatment will make him upset and moody, and he will ask for food all the time, even overnight. The next stage, when we change the medication, he will stop eating, and you will have to beg him to eat. In the first phase, he will get chubby. In the second phase, he will lose weight. And then in the last phase, he will add weight again. He will also lose his hair temporarily while he is receiving chemotherapy, which will grow back afterwards. After we finish the intense treatment, he will go back to his shape within three months. After the intense period of chemotherapy, he will take tablets at home with check-up visits in the hospital every two weeks for eighteen months, which we call "maintenance period".'

We had to wait for about three months until after the day-seventy-nine test to know his risk level and next phases of treatment, such a long and stressful period of waiting.

The chemotherapy lowered his immune system and increased the risk of infection. Children had died because of infection in the past. We had to limit his contact with friends and relatives and watch his temperature all the time. If his temperature would hit thirty-eight degrees, we had to go straight to the hospital emergency and stay in the hospital for forty-eight hours to ensure there was no infection in his blood.

'How can we tell he will be completely cured?' I asked.

'The equipment for the bone marrow test has a defined accuracy. The test may detect no cancerous cells in the body, which we call remission, but this does not necessarily mean there are no cancerous cells left. There is a small chance for residual cancerous cells. Therefore, the treatment takes two years, and we will continue giving him chemotherapy tablets for eighteen months after the intense treatment period,' said Paul.

'What is the chance of a relapse?' asked Emily.

'There is a 20 per cent chance of relapse, which usually happens within one to two years after completion of the maintenance period. After that, the chance is minimal,' said Paul.

I thought to myself that I could choose. I could be a worrying father for a few years, or I could enjoy being with my son and creating joyful moments for him. Lucas deserved to be happy, and I wanted to give him what he would need from his dad.

'Will he become a weak or a normal child after the treatment?' I asked.

'About three months after finishing the intense chemotherapy, he will recover, his hair will grow back, and he will look healthy. His immune system will remain low during the maintenance period because of the side effects of chemotherapy tablets, but not as low as the first six months of the intense chemotherapy. He can have a normal life, but if he gets a temperature, you will need to come to the children's hospital emergency. Six months after the end of the maintenance period, his immune system will also be healthy like everyone else. And he can have a normal life,' said Paul.

This disease may not even affect the full two years of his treatment, but only six months, if there is no complication. So there is hope he could enjoy his childhood and be playful and happy, I told myself.

I hope everything will be fine.

A nurse told us they were transferring Lucas to the oncology ward specialised in children's cancer. At the conscious level, I said to myself that Lucas would be in good hands. But at a subconscious level, I had a terrible feeling about transferring to the oncology ward, which was because of the fear of cancer in public. No matter what I thought or felt, it was what it was, and it was happening to my son. I needed to accept it and deal with it. There was a battle inside me as a father coping with various thoughts and emotions and travelling between conscious and subconscious levels of my mind.

I prayed for Lucas a lot. I was emotional and cried whenever I was alone. Although I did not show it in front of others, and my friends and colleagues kept admiring my strength, I was broken inside. I had never been an emotional person before but, rather, more of a strong rational man. My life had been challenging, but I had never experienced what I was going through. I had changed!

My son had transformed my life and me. My heart was beating for him. I had many plans in my head for him—how we'd enjoy spending time with each other and how I'd teach him life lessons. I wanted to teach him how to ride a bike, how to swim, how to fix things at home, how to make barbecue, and how to play the guitar; help him with his school studies; and, later, teach him how to get a girlfriend. His cancer gave me a bad feeling he would not enjoy all this.

Nevertheless, I kept telling myself to provide positive energy to my son, which was what he needed. I created fun moments for him even while he was in the hospital so he could pass the painful stage of his life.

After they transferred Lucas to his new room, Emily needed to go home to prepare for a more extended stay in the hospital.

When Emily came back to the hospital, she reluctantly told me she had a car accident that had been her fault. She felt embarrassed about the accident in such a situation, but the most important thing was that no one was injured. Only the front left of the car was damaged. I told her not to worry at all, and I was glad she was okay. Considering the pressure on her as a mother, it could be worse. I should have asked someone else to drive her home for her safety.

After only three days, it felt like we had been in the hospital for a long time. It is a human survival strategy—how quickly people adapt themselves to any circumstance.

Most rooms had two beds, and we shared a room with another patient. When we entered the room, we met a six-year-young girl diagnosed with leukaemia one month before Lucas. She was shouting and screaming a lot. The poor little girl was in pain. Her mum felt embarrassed and apologised a few times for the noise her daughter was making.

We learned what was ahead of Lucas! It was not her daughter but the side effects of the steroid. We told her not to worry at all. However, parents usually feel embarrassed in such situations where their child annoys others, no matter what the reason is.

I went to the kitchen to make a coffee and met a man who seemed nervous and restless. He asked me if I was new. I understood that he had been in the hospital for a while. I told him my son had been diagnosed with leukaemia ALL, and it was our third day in the hospital.

He said his four-year-young daughter had high-risk leukaemia AML and would need a bone marrow transplant. His daughter's condition was not looking good. They had been in hospital for over two months. He'd had to quit his work to support his family. The hospital had become their home! He also said AML was harder to treat than ALL.

I felt terrible and did not know what to say. I was devastated myself, but I'd met someone with a worse situation than mine. I sympathised with him. It was an overwhelming but eye-opening conversation.

I came back to the room and told Emily the story. We both thanked God for our situation! Well, we did not know Lucas's risk level yet, but we knew his cancer type was less severe, and there were families around us with much more traumatic situations than ours.

It reminded me of the importance of faith. No matter what my situation is, I should always be grateful for what I have. My son was at least in a stable condition, he was not in pain, and he was conscious and alert. In addition, we were in one of the best children's hospitals in Australia, and my son was in good hands. The treatment was known, and unlike in the 1990s, the cure rate was high. Thank God for all of this.

I hope everything will be fine.

CHAPTER 4

New Job

I decided to start my new job on Monday and assess whether it was the right move, considering our chaotic situation. I was reluctant to return to my previous organisation, but I had to consider all the risks. Family always comes first.

It was Monday morning. I was clean-shaven with my suit and tie on, travelling to the city on the first day of my new contract. It was daunting, unlike my previous projects. I was usually excited about a new challenge. But this time, I was feeling down.

I entered the office and met my direct manager, Jennifer. She sympathised with me and asked about the situation. I found it hard to tell the story. It was as if I did not want to talk about it. I told her the story with difficulty. She was the first one I'd spoken to in person because all the previous days had passed like a flash flood. I'd been too busy to talk to someone and release part of my emotional pressure. She happened to be that person. Sometimes, I had twitching lips and felt embarrassed.

It was not a good way to start a new job, but she better understood the impact of the event on me. I was still in shock and had not recovered yet. She said she well understood the situation, as a relative of hers had gone through cancer and had passed away a few years before.

'I'm not clear about the journey ahead of me. Although I'm excited to rejoin the team for the next phase of the project, I might not be on my full calibre. I have concerns about whether I can focus and deliver to project timelines. I need two weeks to gain more information about my son and determine whether I should stay or return to my previous job,' I told Jennifer.

She accepted this straightaway with respect.

I then met with the rest of the project team, and I liked the team. I started reading the project documentation, and I realised I could not focus at all. I read one page ten times, and I did not understand a word. I felt frustrated. Given the tight project timelines, I had to be quick and responsive. The lack of focus worried me.

My thoughts were with my son. I called Emily many times while I was at work and asked about Lucas. I felt guilty that I was not present in the hospital for Lucas when he needed me.

The first day of my new job passed. I did nothing productive and finished work at three o'clock. I had to finish early and go to the hospital because of a second consultation session about Lucas.

In the meeting, we received information about the treatment plan, risks, and side effects. The team gave us a lot of hope, and I felt more comfortable. The devastating shock and the dreadful image of cancer in our mind had caused so much grief for us. However, the detailed information gave us a more realistic picture of the journey ahead of Lucas and his strong chance of cure.

Emily was upset about the fact that none of the general practitioners had taken her concerns seriously, and they had not investigated further or referred us to a paediatrician. She thought we'd lost some time in the diagnosis. However, in the session, they explained that leukaemia is a rare disease in children, which many general practitioners do not see in their entire career. Besides, the diagnosis was not late, and his condition was under control. The session calmed her down and eased her anger.

I stayed in the hospital until late at night and then went home.

The second day of my new job was not any different from the first day. My mind and heart were with my son, not at work. Wednesday and Thursday were the same and extremely tiring. I came to work at the Sydney CBD early in the morning by bus or train and then went back home, took the car, drove to the hospital, and stayed with Lucas until late at night when he was asleep.

By the time I got home, it was almost midnight. I felt shattered, physically, mentally, and emotionally. Emily stayed with Lucas overnights on weekdays, and I stayed with him on weekends, so Emily could go home and rest.

On Tuesday, 28 February, when I arrived at the hospital after work, I saw a chapel and a book in which parents had written prayers for their children. I wrote a prayer from the bottom of my heart for Lucas to get well soon, have less pain, and return home. Then I went to the oncology ward.

The doctor saw Lucas and was happy with his recovery and what we'd learned on the special care we had to provide him. They sent Lucas home for two days until Friday. The news was amazing!

An image flashed through my mind of the father I'd met in the kitchen whose four-year-young daughter had been in hospital for over two months. I thanked God that Lucas had returned home just after a few days.

I hope everything will be fine.

On Friday, 3 March, Lucas had another operation—a bone marrow test under general anaesthetic—and I could not go to work. My new job was on a daily rate contract. Not being able to work many days would affect my income.

In talking to others in the oncology ward, I learned about the tremendous amount of time some parents had to be present in hospital, which concerned me about my new job. I wanted to be there for my son as much as possible.

In addition, I talked to my workmates, and one of them advised me not to mention my son's treatment to anyone on the project team because some people would take advantage of it against me in the background. He had seen it happen to a friend of his. It is unfortunate that some people are so evil and so much into politics that they would do anything to go up the ladder—even at the price of hurting others and their families.

Considering all this, I emailed Nathan and Laura about my desire to return to my position and the need for their support. Given my knowledge of the project, I could perform well with flexible work arrangements. I was interested in their response and whether they would welcome my return.

On Friday morning, Lucas went through his second operation of the bone marrow test, day eight. I was nervous and prayed all the time. The moment he went to sleep from the anaesthetic in my arms was tough to see. It is hard to say, but I felt I was losing him.

The operation went well, and we needed to wait for the results for a week. Just after the procedure, the first day of his chemotherapy started.

Doctors discharged Lucas for the weekend. They believed it was essential for him to go home and reunite with his imaginary friends and toys to make him happier and avoid depression. He enjoyed playing with his toys in his room. I played with him, and surprisingly, he was full of energy and cheerful.

On Sunday evening, 5 March, Lucas had to be admitted to the hospital again for a few days. Emily asked me to shave his hair before it could start falling out bunch by bunch. In the morning, I cut his hair, having a lot of fun with him, and gave him a good bath. He was ready for the chemotherapy.

As soon as Martin saw Lucas with a shaved head, he asked me to cut his hair too to look like Lucas. He also started fundraising activities at his school for the Leukaemia Foundation.

Emily stayed with Lucas overnight, and I went back home late at night for a rest and to get ready for work on Monday morning.

At work, I could not focus and felt uncomfortable and emotional. I was on the phone a lot talking to Emily about how Lucas was doing in the hospital. I left the workplace early to head back to the hospital and stayed with Lucas until late at night.

On Tuesday, 7 March, I received two emails from Nathan and Laura, who both welcomed my return to my position. I felt peace of mind having read their emails. I decided to return. I would lose extra savings and miss an opportunity for career growth, but supporting my family came first. Career opportunities would present themselves again.

On Wednesday, I let the project team know of my return. They understood my worries and accepted my decision. Emily was also happy with it.

I only worked for two weeks in the new role!

On Friday, 10 March, Lucas had another operation—the day-fifteen bone marrow test. The result was crucial. I felt more comfortable compared to the two previous operations. Seeing my son hooked up to fluids and toxic medication was tough. I often got emotional, but I continuously distracted myself and tried not to think that way, to accept the reality of life, and to focus on making my son happy.

We stayed in the hospital until Saturday evening when they let us go home, which meant Lucas was doing well. On Monday, I was returning to my previous job. I had been to a farewell lunch with my colleagues, and it would be awkward to see me again after only two weeks. I felt secure about my job, but at the same time nervous about my return and the image of me among colleagues.

I think my nervousness was because I was feeling shame about being vulnerable. I had always presented myself as a strong, positive, and happy man, and I did not want others to see the broken side of me. I later understood that nothing is embarrassing about vulnerability. If you embrace it, you can face your deep emotions and manage them much better.

John had asked me to call Centrelink and lodge an application for a healthcare card for Lucas, which would cover a large percentage of the cost of his medication and treatment. I had been swamped and had not called Centrelink. Given the long waiting time on the Centrelink phone queue, I thought I'd call and stay on the line while I was driving to the hospital.

As soon as I called, an automated voice thanked me for calling the disabilities department. I felt horrible, my eyes were full of tears, and I could not phone again. They'd categorised my son as a disable. I did not want to face it.

I waited for a few minutes to feel better, and then drove to the hospital. I never told this to Emily, so that she would not feel bad. I had been protecting her as much as I could.

The day after, when I felt better and more rational than emotional, I called again. And after an hour waiting on the phone, I talked to someone who started the application process.

CHAPTER 5

Next Three Months

On Monday morning, 13 March, I returned to work. Some of my colleagues who did not know the story asked why I'd come back. And those who knew sympathised with me and asked how my little Lucas was doing. Some told me they kept my family in their daily prayers, which I found helpful. It made me think how important it is to be part of a community and have people around when in need.

I had a substantial role in a project. I had some flexibility to work from home or hospital and spend more time with Lucas, which was the main reason I'd returned. Although I was doing well in my role, work politics and dealing with certain characters took a great deal of energy from me and added extra pressure on me.

Lucas remained cheerful most of the time, even when he was in pain and unwell. It is impressive how resilient little ones are. I felt he was striving to stay happy and ignore his limitations.

He reminded me of my early twenties when I'd numbed my emotions not to face my problems. It seems this is a natural human behaviour and a defensive or protective mechanism.

Lucas was getting chubby and puffy because of the side effects of the chemo. He was asking for food all the time, which was challenging to manage, especially for Emily. Overnights, I was waking up many times to feed him and change him. Emily was doing most of it, and she was exceptional. She was not working, which helped her focus on Lucas.

Emily and I had become distant from each other. Our relationship as partners had fallen apart, and there was no intimacy between us. We both were avoiding conflict to keep the peace. Our focus was Lucas. We were not talking about us at all.

I was under a lot of pressure. I was not feeling a relationship with my wife at home. I had worries about buying our first home with crazy property prices in Sydney. My son was going through a hard time. And I had many challenges at work. My dad was ill and, at seventy-three, had depression. My brother had issues with his wife, who had not allowed my mum to see her grandchildren for a while. My mum was feeling lonely and had depression too. My sister was going through a separation from her husband. She wanted to talk to me about her issues, and I tried to listen and help. They were far away from me. I had guilt that I could not be there for them when they needed me.

Family issues had left me feeling sad and brittle. I wished I could go back in time to my childhood moments when I was feeling the joy of life.

I was distressed and cried a lot for my family. Many nights before sleep, I turned my back to Emily in bed and shed tears in quiet. I do not know if she ever noticed it. I had always been the one who kept everyone together in my family, but I had changed. I felt fragile and lonesome. I had never cried like that.

I felt proud of Lucas. He had such a cheerful spirit at the age of two. Nurses adored him and always described him as a happy boy with patience and understanding beyond his age. He was cooperating exceptionally well on such a hard journey. He was cheeky and brought a smile to our faces.

It was late March, and Lucas had put on a few kilos because of the side effects of the steroid. He had joint pain, and it was difficult for him to walk. When he wanted to stand up from a sitting position, he looked like an aged man. I played with him a lot and made him laugh. I think I subconsciously felt I was losing him, and I was striving to create a good time for him as long as he was with me. I also wanted to keep him active and happy so he could overcome the disease.

I always bathed Lucas with lots of play and fun. He liked to play in the water, but he had limitations because of the central line coming out of his chest. I used to take him to the pool to teach him swimming, but I had to stop because of the risk of infection.

We isolated ourselves from visitors, friends, and family because of Lucas's low immune system caused by the chemotherapy. We did not take him out much. He sometimes asked us to do so when we took him for a short walk to a nearby park. I also did not like the way others looked at him because he looked unhealthy.

I noticed that Lucas copied Emily when talking on the phone. It seemed Emily was calling a lot and introducing herself during the day while I was at work, perhaps looking for a job or something else!

On Monday, 27 March, Lucas had another operation for the day-thirty-three bone marrow test. As usual, for the operation, Lucas had to fast from midnight until after the operation in the next morning. It was hard for a little one to be fasting, particularly with his increased appetite caused by the side effects of the steroid.

Hospital rules did not allow more than one person to stay with a child overnight. Emily wanted to stay with Lucas. It would be a long night for both Emily and Lucas. I drove back home around midnight and came back to the hospital the next morning. Emily had red eyes. Lack of sleep had exhausted her.

We took Lucas to the operating room in the OTC (oncology treatment centre). We hugged him and kissed him when they put him to sleep with the anaesthetic. The moment his eyes went to sleep was tough to see. In every operation, tears came to our eyes.

We went out of the operating room. I hugged Emily. She burst into tears. I realised that we had not hugged each other for a while, and that hug was a brief one with no deep connection. We had become strangers in our relationship.

Although I looked okay, I was crushed inside. I felt depressed, confused, and drained. I had been trying all my life to do the right thing and be supportive of my family. But life was getting out of hand. It seemed my life could not settle as I wished it to be, like many of my friends. Life is tough for some and easy for others!

In the hospital, I met families with far worse situations than us. Some of them made me think about how lucky we were. Their lives were a constant battle for the basics everyone had.

A day after the day-thirty-three operation, the second phase of chemotherapy started, which took about a month. A nurse explained the new protocol and medications. We took Lucas to the hospital only once a week as an outpatient. He did not need to stay in the hospital overnight. He could play with toys in the playroom while he received the medication into his blood. Another three days a week, a nurse came home and gave him chemotherapy through his Central Line, which was a five-minute procedure.

Lucas was coping with the chemo very well. According to the oncology doctors, most children lose their hair in this phase of chemotherapy, but he had not lost his hair at all. I thought we had rushed in shaving his hair, but it was okay, he was cute in our eyes.

Emily took Lucas to the hospital, and I had to work. In the oncology clinic, mothers talked about other children. Every time she came back from the hospital, she had a sad story to tell about families and what they went through, which added to the pressure and emotional challenges we had.

On Thursday, 6 April, Lucas had a lumbar puncture operation under anaesthetic in the morning. We went home after the operation. At night, Lucas got a temperature, and we took him to the hospital emergency. It was his first temperature during chemotherapy. He received a blood transfusion and antibiotics. He stayed for two nights in the hospital for his temperature to go down. Doctors ensured he had no infection and then discharged him forty-eight hours after the last recorded temperature of thirty-eight degrees.

Lucas's birthday was on 2 May. We planned for a small birthday party. He was not looking healthy. Nevertheless, we did not want to skip his birthday party. On Saturday, 29 April, we held a birthday party for Lucas, which was not as enjoyable as I expected but was positive after all. I worked hard to have decent decorations, which looked great. We took memorable photos with friends and family. Lucas played with other kids and had a good time. I had grown a beard for some unknown reason; well perhaps subconsciously I was showing my sadness. I had a beard in all the photos, which I wish I did not. Emily hated a beard on my face!

Every week, the central line dressing had to be cleaned and changed. Lucas was amazingly cooperative in allowing the nurses to do their job with ease. I felt proud of him. Nurses always said how brave he was for his age.

On Thursday, 11 May, Lucas had the day-seventy-nine operation of the bone marrow test. The day-seventy-nine test results, combined with the other test results, would confirm his risk level. We needed to wait for two weeks for the test result.

Friday, 12 May, was Mother's Day. I thought to surprise Emily with something special. I felt a relaxing massage would be what she needed. She loved massage. I came home from work and put the flowers outside to surprise her, and I arranged for Lucas to give the gifts to her. It worked out well, and we surprised her!

She is a great mum and deserves happiness, but I cannot give her what she deserves at the moment, I thought to myself.

Lucas's third phase of chemotherapy started on 23 May, which comprised four blocks of four days each as an inpatient in the hospital. Lucas had to receive fluids for forty-eight hours continuously. It was so hard to keep a two-year-young boy on a hospital bed for three days.

He lost his appetite and all the weight he had gained. We had to change his nappy many times because of the continuous fluid he was receiving. I worked on weekdays and, after work, came to the hospital to take over from Emily until late at night. On weekends, I stayed overnight, and Emily went home for a rest.

Most rooms had two beds, and we often shared a room with other parents. A Chinese family came to our room with their daughter, who'd been diagnosed with leukaemia. They were both in shock, but Dad's emotional state was worse. They asked questions about Lucas and his treatment plan. I felt we had to leave it to the doctors to provide the right information to them. Each child's condition might be different. In addition, the timing of providing information matters when parents are in shock. Doctors and nurses know better when and how to give information to parents.

Paul came to our room to give us the day-seventy-nine test results. My heart was pounding to know the outcome. His test result was excellent. The treatment had been effective on Lucas, and his risk level was not high. Therefore, Lucas would not need a bone marrow transplant, which was great news. Emily and I both had tears in our eyes, but happy tears.

The Chinese family heard the good news about Lucas, which gave them hope for their daughter. They felt much better, and a smile appeared on their faces. Hope had made them happier.

However, it did not last long for them. A day after, they received terrible news that their daughter's risk level was high; hence, she needed more intense treatment and a bone marrow transplant. They were sad, quiet, and kept to themselves. I felt they compared their situation to ours and asked themselves, *Why my daughter?* It's a naive question we all ask when life gets tough.

After a while, they started talking to us and asking questions again. Mum was so nervous and burst into tears. I hugged her and sympathised with her, which helped her calm down. I thought, although we were going through a hard journey, compared to many others, we were still lucky.

Four blocks of chemotherapy of the third phase went well for Lucas. He was still holding onto his hair, which was rare. He had lost a lot of weight, and he looked less chubby but not skinny. I saw scrawny children at that phase. Lucas was coping exceptionally well. The third phase would end in the middle of July, and then the last and the most intense one would begin.

Although I had been under pressure at work because of the workload and workplace politics, I had been present for my son at all stages of his treatment in the hospital. I was proud of myself as a father.

Edward had asked me a few times to go to the city for a drink. I did go to Sydney pubs with him, but it did not feel right, and I could not enjoy it. I think subconsciously I did not permit myself to enjoy anything outside of spending time with my son while he was suffering. In addition, my deteriorated relationship with Emily added to my frustration.

I used to barbeque on weekends and in picnics. Emily loved my meat sticks on a wood fire. However, I had lost my passion for life. I had lost my sense of enjoyment. Emily had asked me many times to set up a charcoal grill, the same as before, but I was not in the mood. I said okay to her every time she asked, but I put it in the back of my mind.

I tried to approach Emily to talk about our relationship, but I could not. A few times, Emily started the conversation about us, but I stayed quiet and avoided the conversation, or answered briefly.

'You are not treating me well,' said Emily.

'I'm sorry you feel that way, but I'm just into myself these days,' I replied.

'Do you still love me?' said Emily.

'I cannot feel anything,' I replied honestly, as I genuinely could not feel anything.

I think I did not mean to say I did not love Emily. I meant to say my senses and feelings were shut down, and I was emotionally numb because I was distressed and depressed.

This conversation happened only once. That night, I felt awful inside. I had always been kind to her and treated her well. However, she felt frustrated in our relationship.

I feared potential arguments, which could lead to a big fight. I was not confident about my feelings. I was worried I'd say something I regretted, so I preferred to stay quiet. We had a few small arguments over minor issues; I felt we were ready for a big fight. I tried not to trigger that until we had passed the hard stage of our life.

I hope everything will be fine.

❖

CHAPTER 6

My Marriage

On Monday, 10 July, when I came home from work, Emily told me, 'I can still love you,' and a few statements I cannot clearly remember.

It sounded unusual. It was not clear to me what she meant and what I was supposed to do or say. I said nothing because I was cautious not to say something harmful. I was not confident about my thoughts and feelings, so I stayed quiet. Emily did not insist on continuing the conversation either. It seemed she had the same fears as mine.

On Tuesday, 11 July, when I was driving home from work, Edward called me and said he needed to talk to me and insisted on going to a bar for a drink. It was odd. This had never happened. I called Emily, and she did not pick up the phone. I was puzzled as I considered what it could be about. Some negative thoughts about Lucas flashed through my mind, but I quickly distracted myself and tried to stay positive.

We went to a bar in Crows Nest, and after a few minutes of chat, he let me know that Emily had left me and he was just made aware of it. Emily had done it in quiet without her family knowing.

'She needs to be separate for a while and has rented a place nearby. She needs space for a few months to see if you can get back together,' said Edward.

I initially felt angry with her, mainly because of Lucas. His face—suffering from all the things happening to him—was the first picture in my head.

How could she do this at the beginning of the most intense period of Lucas's chemotherapy? Is the pain and suffering he is going through not enough? And he has to be taken away from his father too? I asked myself.

I calmed myself down, and I told myself that I had to be cautious about every single action to protect my son from any harm. What was done was done. I could not change the past. Lucas needed my support, which was the most important thing. I had to minimise the impact on him.

Many children take the blame for family separations in their mind without saying it. Kids need to feel loved by their parents. They should never feel guilty about the issues between their parents.

I went home. When I opened the door, the home was half-empty. She had taken half of the homeware. I called her; she did not answer. I realised I had received a text message from the bank that Emily had withdrawn half of the money from our shared bank account. I anxiously checked my bag in which I kept the identity documents and noticed she had taken Lucas's birth certificate and passport.

I realised why Lucas had copied Emily introducing herself on the phone. Emily had been planning this for weeks. I felt betrayed and plotted against.

The weekend before she left, we had gone shopping and bought two new towels, one for me and one for

Emily. The pictures of us choosing what we liked passed through my mind, and I felt like a fool. *All that time, she was telling lies. How could she look into my eyes while she had arranged everything to leave me?* I thought to myself.

I stepped back and sat down on the floor for a few seconds and then jumped up and sprinted to Lucas's bedroom. The door to his room was ajar. I paused and slowly opened the door. Emily had wiped out Lucas's bedroom and had left none of his belongings or toys. I knelt on my knees and felt she had kicked me out of their lives. I felt empty. A large Mickey Mouse plush doll I had bought for Lucas with so much love was the first image that passed through my mind. I pressed my forehead against the floor and closed my eyes for many minutes.

What about me? Don't fathers have a heart? What happens when Lucas misses me and wants my cuddles? We have always been honest with each other. We could have talked about our separation and planned for it to minimise the impact on all of us. What should I do now? Various thoughts ran through my head.

I could not see my son that night, and I did not know where my family was. I was in a massive shock and sobbed all night like a baby. I felt broken, lost, and devastated. I repeatedly called myself a failure in life. I had never felt that way. I had always felt successful and positive.

I went to work the next morning as if nothing had happened. I was in shock and distressed.

When I arrived at the office, I pulled myself together and sent Emily a video message with a smile and gentle tone to ease her anxiety and worries: 'Hi, Emily. I hope everything is okay. I think we had to do this. We need to talk, but we should focus on supporting Lucas. Please let me know if you need anything.'

'Thanks for your message. It made Lucas happy. I am busy now. Have a good day,' texted Emily and sent me her address.

It turned out she had rented a small apartment 500 metres away from our place. She had chosen a place close by, so I could support Lucas.

I had a morning session with Kevin, the new project executive. He was the first person I met after the shock. At the end of our meeting, I told him the distressful news. I was emotional and had twitching lips when I said it. Kevin was not sure how to react to the terrible news. I made a horrible first impression on the new executive, which would create unease in our working relationship.

I was in shock, confused, and lost in life. My head was full of noise, and I could not focus. I perhaps could not do better. Well, I should not have gone to work a day after a massive shock—an act that, in itself, was a sign of being in shock.

After the meeting, I went to make a coffee. There, I saw Peter who was a senior manager. He always empathised with me about my son's health. As soon as he saw me, he said I looked pale. I told him the story with an emotional expression on my face, which he told me about later.

I had another meeting after the coffee where a young consultant announced his marriage and showed us gorgeous pictures of his wedding ceremony. What a strange world! On a day when I was feeling miserable, another person was experiencing moments of utter bliss. I had been in that happy state before, showing the pictures of my wedding and my son's first few days to friends and colleagues.

I thought to myself that, when I had expressed my happiness with pride and joy, other people around me might have been in a traumatic situation. Nothing is wrong with showing emotions, either sadness or happiness, but knowing how to express them would help avoid emotional discomfort for others.

I left work early and went home. My head felt heavy, and I needed to rest. Nathan called and sympathised with me and offered his support, which was nice. But what kind of help would I need?

After a rest, I pulled myself together and went to Emily's new apartment to see my son. I pretended nothing had happened, to protect Lucas. I played with him and installed their shower so they could take a warm bath, and then I put my son to sleep while singing lullaby songs for him, as usual.

Once Lucas went to sleep, I left Emily's place. We did not get into a conversation. I think both of us feared a potential argument, which would put stress on Lucas.

It was a short walk from her apartment to my place. I walked while I was crying. I felt I'd failed to hold my family together.

When I got home, I cried my eyes out all night, yelling at God and myself until I fell asleep with a massive headache. In talking to God, I complained about the trauma I was experiencing. I shouted, 'Why?' I was rude to God. I ordered him, 'I want my life back!' I was harsh on me and called myself horrible things. I felt disdain for myself.

Although I am not religious, I believe in God. When I was a teenager, I was closer to God. I loved God and often spoke to him, intimately and joyfully. However, after my dad's bankruptcy, which turned our beautiful life into a battle for basics, I became disconnected from God. One might think life's challenges get you closer to God, but I do not believe it is true.

Have I turned my back on God because I am upset about how God allowed the destruction of my lovely family? Is God punishing me, by destroying my family again, to teach me I have to accept my destiny, whatever it is, and still be grateful? Or are these just random incidents, and I am just unlucky? Or is it me? Am I unable to manage my life? I think it is all my fault, I thought to myself.

I have friends who do not even believe in God, but life has been kind to them. Why is life so tough on some but gentle on others? Are these events the act of God or random incidents? How much of what happens is in our hands? The bankruptcy of my dad, cancer of my son, and the sudden departure of my wife—I had no control over any of these shocking disasters. But, yes, I

could control how I responded to them. How have I responded?
Could I have done anything differently?

I was going mad with all the thoughts in my spinning head. I had a constant headache most of the time.

How could I protect my son as his father if I was not present in his life?

Lucas had become everything in my life. It broke my heart that he had been taken away from a loving dad, and I had no control over it. Life was out of my hands and far too strong for me to take control.

On Wednesday, 13 July, I sent a text message to Emily:

> Dear Emily,
>
> I am sorry I haven't understood you and haven't supported you. I have been too much into myself. I am in shock and concerned about your well-being. You have told Edward that I do not want you any longer, but it is not true. You have misunderstood me. I have just been into myself. I have always loved you. I always wanted us to build our life together. You

are worth a world to me. I suggest you
come back home after a few weeks.
Many months of separation may break
our relationship further. We should
speak more often. I will look after you.
If you would like, we can get counselling
too. Please let me know.

'I'll think about it. I need time,' replied Emily.

I told my family and close friends that Emily had
left me. They could not believe it based on the picture
they had in mind from our close relationship. Emily was
reluctant to tell others about our separation. She was
hiding it from most of her relatives and friends.

When my mum and dad heard the news of our
separation, they felt devastated. They had a tough life
and did not find happiness in their relationship. They
wanted to see their children happy, but we all had issues.

My dad never recovered from those painful years of
bankruptcy, and he got very ill physically, mentally, and
emotionally over time. He passed away at seventy-five,
on 10 July 2019, two years after the time of this book.
When he passed away, he was looking twenty years
older than his age. We had a close father-and-son bond,

and his passing was painful for me. However, I felt he was relieved from enduring emotional pain. I tried to help him move on from his past, but he could not.

When he passed away, I got a constant headache for a few days until I made a small wooden raft with candles and flowers on it and put it on a Sydney river to bid Dad farewell with a wish to free his soul. It calmed me down.

I wrote a letter to my dad:

> I am sad not because you left, as you are relieved from constant pain. I'm sad because I wasn't with you when you needed me. I'm sorry, Dad. I know you have called for me in the last few minutes of your life. I sensed it miles away from you. I'm sorry I wasn't there for you. I miss your warm voice and the way you always looked at me full of a fatherly love. I love you. Rest in peace.

My father was a dedicated family man who gave his unconditional love to his children. He believed life is all about family. However, he failed in holding his family together. He could not let go of the feelings of failure and shame. It was weird that the same had happened to me! I told myself not to follow my dad's footsteps—to let go of the past and move on. I hoped I could!

Back to July 2017, when I was alone, I cried a lot. I was missing my son, in a home empty of love and the joy brought by my little boy. Most nights, I slept with a heavy head and swollen eyes. I must have looked awful in the eyes of others.

I felt lost without Emily and Lucas, but I wanted to minimise the impact on my son. I tried not to let Lucas sense my busted-up self. However, he sensed my sadness. A few times, he said to me, 'Are you happy, Daddy?' and then hugged me.

I had always aimed at maintaining a balance in my life, and I had managed it well until my life turned into a mess suddenly. I had always come home early, rather than staying at work for long hours, to spend quality time with my wife and son. My family had always been my priority, but I had lost my family. Love of family makes the life marrow, and without it, life would be brittle. I could not see myself happy again without my family. Home, family, and love bring joy and happiness.

Our family is not something we choose in life, but we should embrace our loved ones just as they are. Nothing and nobody is perfect, but our family keeps everyone together. It gives us love, joy, hope, and desire for life.

On the night I was rude to God, I felt what had happened to me—a kind and honest family man—was unfair. I had the same feeling when life brutally crushed my parents, good loving people. Well, life is not fair anyway. Fairness is a naive expectation we all have from life.

When I left the office on weekdays, I was confused about where to go. I did not want to go to an empty home, but I could not impose myself on Emily, who had left me. Equally, I was Lucas's father and wanted to be a good dad. He needed me, and I needed him too. It was a horrible situation.

What have I done that I deserve this? Emily believes we could not continue living together, but does she understand the impact of the way she left—without even talking to me? And the damage on our son and me?" I talked to myself more and more, full of confusion and mixed feelings.

The disgraceful way Emily had left me upset me. I felt she had betrayed my son, our life, and me. Her act had damaged my feelings, and I could not fix it. Many times I looked at our pictures and tried to remember how I loved Emily, but I could not bring back the feeling of love for her. I was emotionally numb.

I've only been into myself. I haven't hurt her or done anything wrong. We have been distant, but shouldn't have we tried to work things out before blowing everything up? Shouldn't have we talked about our separation and agreed on terms before doing it? I thought to myself.

I asked Emily why she had never talked to me about her feelings before she left me. She answered that she had tried, but I had never listened. Apparently, I had not heard her. I had been too much into myself and ignorant of her needs and feelings.

Too many men go quiet in their caves for a long time to deal with their issues all alone, even at the toughest times. Women talk to each other and share their feelings, which helps them reflect on their emotions much better than men, I believe.

I asked Emily why she had concealed such an important decision for our life, and why she had done it abruptly. She answered that she could not tell me. She said it was hard for her, but she had to do it.

Edward said to me that Emily had felt I did not love her anymore, and she had thought I wanted to leave her, so she'd left. I had never thought about leaving her. However, when I asked myself if I loved her, I paused, and I could not feel love. So her feeling was correct, but I did not know why I was feeling nothing except the love for my son. I thought how I'd used to love Emily, and I did not know what had happened to my love for her.

Those days I slept a lot, closed my eyes for a long time. I did not have enough energy to be the same active man I used to be. In the mornings, I woke up very hard. I was depressed and anxious, which I had never experienced before in my life. I was well aware of what was happening to me, but I could not do anything about it. Time was perhaps the solution. I was trying to hold up and be there for my son. That was all that mattered to me.

I called my friend Sam and let him know that Emily had left me.

'It is shocking. I had no such impression about your relationship. Do not ruin your lives. You are both experiencing trauma. Emily did the wrong thing. You are a reasonable man. She should have talked to you. She has been under extreme pressure. Can you forgive her and get back together?' asked Sam.

A week after our separation, on Wednesday, 19 July, Lucas had a heart echo test to check whether he was ready for the rest of the treatment. A few days later, the last phase of the intense chemotherapy started. The fourth phase of chemo was the most intense protocol, which took two months. We only needed to go to the hospital once a week, with no overnight stay unless Lucas would get temperature. We were lucky that he had got temperature only once. Most kids get temperature a few times during chemotherapy.

I was going to all hospital appointments with Lucas, regardless of how busy I was. Lucas had to take the steroid on a higher dose. The steroid made him chubby again, even more than the first phase had. He started losing his hair, and I saw a lot of hair on his pillow. He was suffering a lot. He had pain, especially in his knees. He was breathing harder and walking with unease, but he still asked me to take him out for a walk. Lucas was such a resilient and lively boy.

I was having a hard time. Work was hectic, and the project was putting pressure on me. My personal life was in a mess. I had no place of warmth and peace, and I was under constant stress. I was living in a colourless home with no sound of family and half empty of homeware. Every time I sat on the couch, the pictures of Lucas playing and the memories I had with him passed through my mind and made me emotional. Sometimes, I heard his voice from his room in my head.

I decided to get rid of the bed, couch, and table, which gave me negative feelings. I posted them online for sale with low prices or free. Many buyers contacted me, and in only a few days, I'd sold them all.

I was then living in an empty place like a ghost house, a home with no spirit and sound of love and family. I hated that place, and I wanted to move out as soon as possible.

I decided to purchase a small apartment for myself and become more stable to better support my son. It was likely for Sydney house prices to fall within a year, and my commercial instinct was telling me to wait. However, life was pushing, and my heart was telling a different story. I felt I had to be in a position of stability to be a good dad for my son. I wanted to create a place of love and comfort for Lucas to enjoy spending time with me.

I applied for a home loan and searched for a place. On weekends, I took Lucas with me to home inspections. I made it adventurous and fun for him.

In the middle of all that, I had a project management certification exam at the end of August, which I had enrolled in previously. It was hard to focus on my study, given all the mental and emotional pressure I had. However, I wanted to achieve my target plans.

On Saturday, 19 August, I saw a place I liked. It was a small apartment but spacious compared to an apartment. I felt good about it. It gave me a positive vibe. I knew it was not a good time to buy, but I did not care. My priority was to create a home for myself and ensure my son felt secure, safe, and happy at his daddy's place. I made an offer and put together documentation for the final approval of the home loan.

On Friday, 25 August, I went to the Sydney CBD for the exam. There was a pre-exam course in the morning and the exam in the afternoon. I was ready for the exam. Before noon, Emily called to tell me that Lucas had a temperature, and she was taking him to the hospital emergency. I felt nervous and shared this with the course instructor. He recommended not to take the exam and to postpone it for another time. It was a three-hour exam, and focus was essential. Initially, I agreed with him, but I told myself not to rush, as I felt in my heart that it was nothing serious with Lucas. After an hour, I called Emily again.

'Lucas is well, and everything is under control, but he has to stay in the hospital for forty-eight hours to ensure there is no infection in his blood,' said Emily.

The news was a relief for me. I took the exam and passed it. At around four o'clock, I went to the hospital and stayed with Lucas until late at night. At around midnight, I headed back to my empty home and slept on the floor. I drank alcohol a lot that night. When I was drunk, I wailed my wretched life on the floor of my empty bedroom. I needed to release the accumulated pressure.

I talked to God when I was drunk. This time, I was polite to God but still hard on myself. I needed an answer. I asked God what to do. I asked for light, since I had lost my way in life, and I did not know what to do.

'God, please show me the way. I desperately need help.'

My son had lost all his hair, and his face looked unhealthy. But in my eyes, he was beautiful, and his smile made me happy. His voice sounded weak and scratchy, but I enjoyed listening to him. I often recorded his voice and listened to the recordings when I was alone.

His temperature was not coming down, and he had to stay in the hospital for eight days. His blood count was low, and he needed a blood transfusion. I stayed with him in the hospital for three nights. The nights I stayed with Lucas, I made it fun for him. I took him for a walk in the hospital garden with all the equipment attached to him and played with him. Lucas liked the garden, its small waterfall, and a pond of fish.

Lucas often wanted to push the IV rack himself and be self-sufficient. Nurses found him different from other kids. They said it to me multiple times. He cooperated extremely well with nurses without crying and screaming, which, according to them, kids much older than him did not. I felt proud of him.

He was in isolation in a private room and prohibited from having any visitors because of his deficient immunity and risk of infection. He loved Thomas and Friends train stories. I brought him a small battery-operated Thomas and Friends train set to play while stuck in the hospital bed. He spent hours playing with Thomas and Percy. I enjoyed watching him and playing with him. Lucas stayed in the hospital until Friday, 1 September, on which he had an ultrasound test. The result was excellent, and he went home.

I went to Emily's place for a couple of hours every day to spend time with Lucas. On Sunday, 3 September, when I went to Emily's apartment to see Lucas, they surprised me for Father's Day with presents—a cup with 'No. 1 Dad' written on it, flowers, and chocolate. Although I liked it and appreciated Emily, I did not feel the genuine happiness I used to feel. I felt dejected. Emily's place gave me negative energy and depressing feelings.

On Wednesday, 6 September, Lucas got another temperature, and we had to stay in the hospital for three days. I stayed a night with Lucas. He was in an isolated private room. I played music for him on my phone, and we drew colourful pictures. I rolled the pencils down the table, and before they fell from the table onto the bed, I snatched them in the air. This play was funny for Lucas. He guffawed every time I caught the pencil. Good laughter made our eyes wet. I recorded a video of our memorable moments, and we watched it back together. I then told a bedtime story for him until he closed his tired yet cheerful eyes. Staying in the hospital did not stop us from creating happy moments. Every second was worth a world.

I hope everything will be fine.

✦•◆

CHAPTER 7

End of Treatment

On 7 and 14 September, Lucas had two operations under general anaesthetic. On Monday, 18 September, he received his last dose of chemotherapy, which concluded the intense phase of treatment.

Paul examined him and was happy with the test results and his condition. He told us he could start the maintenance period straightaway in a few days. I felt delighted, and happy tears came to my eyes. Lucas had passed a hard stage and had survived.

It would take three to six months for him to recover from the side effects of chemotherapy—for his hair to grow back, for his chubby face to look healthy, and for him to be able to walk and run like other kids.

I had to move into my new place in two weeks on 30 September. I packed the rest of my stuff and started searching for homeware to build a new home from scratch. I wanted to create a place of warmth and love for Lucas to enjoy spending time with his dad. Browsing shops for appliances and furniture by myself felt unusual, as I had always been with my family when doing these things. The pictures of Emily and me when we were moving together kept passing through my mind.

On Thursday, 21 September, Lucas was unwell and felt tired. Emily called the children's hospital and provided the symptoms. They advised the symptoms were common after the most intense phase of chemotherapy. However, her instinct told her a different story. She called me, explained her concerns, and said she wanted to take him straight to the hospital emergency. I supported her feelings and told her I was going too. I felt worried.

I had a meeting with my project team at two o'clock to plan for the next week of software testing activities. I was very nervous during the session. My colleagues had no idea what was going through my mind and how much pressure I was experiencing at work.

It reminded me how important it is to be compassionate and considerate of our friends and colleagues at all times, because we may not know what they are going through. It is essential to have empathy and be careful in our tone and language not to cause stress and unease for others.

After the meeting, I ran out of the office and drove to the hospital, my eyes full of tears. I sensed something was not right, but I kept telling myself to stay positive.

When I arrived, Lucas was in the room at the end of the hallway of the oncology ward. He saw me when I was approaching the room. His eyes went wet, and his lips had a twitch. As soon as I entered the room, he said, 'Daddy, cuddle me,' and burst into tears.

I hugged him hard. He put his head on my shoulder for a few minutes and felt much better.

Lucas was feeling unwell, and he was in pain. He was breathing with difficulty. His belly had become larger than usual in one day. A doctor examined him and booked him for an emergency ultrasound.

In the ultrasound waiting room, Lucas could not keep his eyes open and was not responsive. He closed his eyes, and when I talked to him, he did not answer. He was not himself. I had not seen him like that in the whole period of chemotherapy. I had a horrible feeling that I was losing my son.

I was shivering and could not stop my tears. I noticed other parents were looking at us with tears in their eyes. The nurse's expression as she looked at Lucas worried me more, because it was clear she knew something was wrong.

Emily and I felt scared but barely talked to each other because of our deteriorated relationship. We could not support each other at such a hard time. What a shame!

After the ultrasound, we went back to the room in the oncology ward. We waited for doctors to let us know the test result. It was daunting and distressful.

We shared a room with a lovely family. Their twelve-year-young son, Jacob, was suffering and having a hard time. He was a cute boy with a warm and loving family. The period of staying with them was a pleasure for us.

A junior doctor saw us and gave us the bad news that Lucas had been diagnosed with a liver dysfunction called VOD, or veno-occlusive disease, a rare side effect of chemotherapy. The doctor said we would need to stay in the hospital for two weeks for the treatment. Lucas could not start the maintenance period until they had treated the disease.

The doctor did not transfer the message well and gave us a massive shock, perhaps because of lack of experience. Emily burst into tears. We felt we were losing Lucas. We felt devastated again.

A while later, Paul and Sharon saw us and explained the disease in more detail. They believed the disease was treatable. But if not, it could end his life.

Just when we were feeling delighted that we had reached the end of the intense period of chemotherapy and Lucas could experience relief from pain, more shocking news snatched our happiness. It reminded me of how fragile happiness can be. Anyway, I had to remain hopeful to support my wonderful son.

Lucas could not breathe normally. His tummy had become massive and hard. He was in a lot of pain and had to take strong painkillers. I was distressed, and sometimes, the picture of his death crossed my mind. What a terrible feeling!

Watching him suffer that much and not able to do anything for him was heartbreaking. I could not sleep well, had nightmares, and woke up a few times in the middle of the night. I often felt exhausted.

I was weary of being in shock. I only hoped everything would be fine.

I stayed with Lucas in the hospital during the weekend. He got much better in two days. His excellent responsiveness to the treatment was unexpected for his doctors.

Such a huge relief!

They allowed Lucas to go home on Sunday evening, 25 September. However, he had to take his medication at home for another two weeks. His medication had to flow into his blood all the time continuously, so they gave him a portable infusion pump connected to his central line, which he had to carry like a bag hanging from his shoulder. He was such a tolerant little boy. He understood the situation well and did not complain at all. We had to wait for his liver function to get healthy to start the maintenance period in which he would need to continue taking chemotherapy tablets for eighteen months.

The following week was hectic. I went to Wollongong for three days, from 26 to 28 September with my project team. After I returned to Sydney, I moved into my new place on Friday, 29 September.

On Saturday, I cleaned the apartment and unpacked my stuff in the morning. Then I went to the hospital and stayed with Lucas on Saturday and Sunday. We had a private room.

In the evening, I played classical guitar music on my mobile from Barrios, a genius in songwriting for guitar. I had joyful moments with Lucas. We had so much fun, and I made him laugh a lot. I took a video of our lovely father-and-son moments.

He did not sleep until about eleven o'clock that night, which was very late for a two-year-young boy. I think having fun with his dad was keeping him awake until late. He went to sleep much earlier when he was with Emily.

Lucas got much better, and his liver function returned normal. On Wednesday, 4 October, doctors removed the portable device and gave us the instructions and medication to start the maintenance period.

Lucas had to take chemo tablets every night for eighteen months. Doctors advised the medicine would be most effective if given late at night. We dissolved the tablets in two milligrams of water in a syringe and injected it into his mouth at around ten o'clock while he was asleep. Well, we had to wake him up a bit, so he could swallow.

The medicine had a horrible taste like iron. It felt as if I was poisoning my son. The chemotherapy tablets kept his immune system low during the maintenance period. We had to watch his temperature for the risk of infection.

He was free from that heavy bag hanging from him all the time. He was happier he could run around again—well, not quite there yet. He still had the central line, which they had planned to remove in a few weeks when his stability was well assured. It would take at least three months for his face to look healthy again. I could not wait to take Lucas to the beach during the Christmas holidays and spend time with him playing on the sand.

I hope everything will be fine.

CHAPTER 8

Daddy's Place

I told Emily I'd bought a place for myself and moved in. She did not like it and looked furious, but then she asked a few questions about it. I felt secure rather than fragile, which was what I needed as a father to support my lovely Lucas. I would let nothing impact our beautiful father-and-son relationship. I would always be there for him.

I had no homeware and not much stuff other than a few boxes, bags, clothes, my guitar, and a kayak. The apartment had no lock-up garage but a parking spot for a car, not boats. I had to put my kayak next to my car for a short period until I figured out what to do with it.

It was a high-quality double kayak. I had good memories of it, paddling with Emily. I had thought about paddling in the middle of beautiful Sydney rivers and bays with Lucas. However, I did not have space to keep it.

Well, when I faced my emotions, I wanted to get rid of it because I was upset about Emily. Otherwise, I could have kept it at a friend's house.

I took some pictures of it and posted it online for sale. I'd have years to buy two new kayaks and paddle with Lucas.

On Saturday, 14 October, I took Lucas to my new apartment for the first time. The apartment was empty of furniture. He enjoyed playing and running in an empty apartment. I was playing guitar, Lucas was singing along with me, and I was recording our voices when Emily called to talk to him.

'I am at Daddy's home. This is Lucas's home,' said Lucas.

I felt great about how Lucas felt about me and that we had such a robust father-and-son bond between us. I believe subconsciously I felt I'd failed when it came to holding my family together, but I was trying to prove to myself that I was a good father.

One day when I was driving home from Emily's place with Lucas in my car, he said he had forgotten to take his drawer with him to Daddy's place. He had pictured himself moving in and living with me. Initially, I was not sure how to respond. Then I explained to him he had two homes and did not need to move anything out from his mum's place. He could have everything at Daddy's place too. He quickly understood and accepted. I wanted to spend quality time with Lucas and be a great dad for him.

I had arranged for changing the carpet to floorboards in a few weeks and buying furniture. Until then, Lucas could not stay overnight at my place. I did not even have a fridge.

On Thursday, 2 November, Lucas had his central line removed, which was a simple operation under general anaesthetic. Emily and I were both thrilled to see Lucas free from the tube dangling from his chest. He would be free to swim and play with other children again.

When he was put to sleep with anaesthetic, only one parent could go with him in the operating room. Emily wanted to be with Lucas, but he cried and asked me to stay with him. He grabbed my hand hard and did not want to let go.

The anaesthetist made an exception and let us both in the operating room with Lucas. While I had taken Lucas's hand and his beautiful eyes were going to sleep, I prayed for it to be his last operation. He had endured fourteen medical operations, and this was his fifteenth. Well, he would have one more operation at the end of the maintenance period, around March 2019.

The only downside of removing his central line was that for every fortnightly blood test for the next seventeen months, he would receive a needle in his arm to take a blood sample.

Nevertheless, he was absolutely fine with it. He watched the nurse when taking blood from his arm, looked at me with pride, and said, 'Did you see I didn't cry?'

I felt proud of him—such a brave and understanding boy.

By the end of October, I finished the renovations and bought homeware and toys for Lucas. I saw colourful beds for kids, and I liked a sailor bunk bed and a blue car bed. I got too excited and bought the bunk bed without doing enough research. During the week after work, I installed it all by myself, which was quite hard. I wished for Lucas to stay with me on weekends.

On Friday, 3 November, I went to Emily's place and took Lucas to my apartment. I was excited to see his reaction to his bunk bed. He enjoyed going upstairs and downstairs, and when he was on the bed, he looked like he had conquered the world.

Then he started jumping on the bed! I got worried that he would fall from the bed. It was not safe. I took a video and emailed it to the store I'd bought it from and asked if I could return it. Lucas slept on my bed that night, since I could not trust leaving him on the bunk bed.

The store manager responded that the minimum age for a bunk bed is nine, and it was my responsibility to research before buying. Still, I believed they should have mentioned the age limit for their product both in the store and on their website, which they added later.

Eventually, the store manager accepted the return with an 80 per cent refund. I uninstalled it all alone, which was a backbreaking effort and replaced it with a car bed.

The following weekend, Lucas looked for his bunk bed and asked me about what had happened to it. But he loved his car bed too and soon forgot the bunk bed.

Lucas spent most weekends with me. I had settled at my place and had everything arranged for Lucas to have a good time at his daddy's place.

Lucas was with Emily during the week and with me on weekends, which had become my routine. On weekdays, I felt depressed when I returned home. I had always left work excited to get home and spend time with my wife and son. However, there was no sound of a family at home any longer. I had never lived alone before. I had always lived with either family or friends. I was wondering how some people live alone!

Many times, when I was alone, I convinced myself to ask Emily if she would consider getting back together and rebuilding our family. However, whenever I saw her, I could not tell her. I even struggled with maintaining eye contact with her. I no longer trusted her. When she talked to me, I escaped the conversation and played with Lucas.

I felt heartbroken. I think I was angry with her for the way she'd left me. I also felt shame as a man because I had not made her happy, and I had let her down. Sometimes, I felt hatred for her because she had taken Lucas away from me. I was confused, with mixed feelings and fluctuating emotions. My heart was empty of love for a woman.

Some friends believed we had to get back together, but I was not optimistic about our ability to rebuild our broken relationship, love, and trust. Others told me to find a new partner, but I did not feel ready to move on. I felt guilty if I looked after myself while my son needed me.

Most nights, when I came home, I either worked or wrote this book for a few hours and then went to bed. In writing this book, I rewound my memories in detail, watched our family photos and videos, read the text messages with Emily, and reviewed my notes to capture events as they had happened. Writing this book brought back all the memories and put extra emotional pressure on me. I cried a lot. Nevertheless, I wanted to finish this book. Writing helped me face my feelings, and I grew through pain.

I felt others were staying away from me. It even upset me that some friends had not asked how I was doing. But it was me who'd pushed everyone away. They might have thought I needed space.

I stayed away from my friends and relatives, because of a strong feeling of shame, I believe. I followed the same traits as my early twenties. I had not learned a crucial lesson that resilience is the ability to maintain internal happiness at the toughest times. In fact, I had not become resilient enough yet. I had isolated myself because I had no courage to face my vulnerability and share it with other people. There is no shame in failure and vulnerability.

I was tired of trying to settle my life, which started when my father took risks and was bankrupt. I think I lost my way right there, and I had been searching to find a life since. The key reason for my unhappiness was my mindset and expectations based on my past lifestyle, which had changed. I could not adjust my expectations and adapt to the new circumstances. It led to disappointment and frustration. I was constantly running after a life I had in mind.

There are two kinds of people—those who take a safe and known path, and those who take risks and try unknown off-road paths, which may turn into a triumph or failure. In taking risks, some people get lost in life, and it might take years for them to get back on track. I believe my dad took an off-road path to where he was lost and never found his way.

Life is like a puzzle in which everyone has a place. Those who find their place live a happy life, and those who are misplaced remain in a chase to find themselves. Resilience, control, zest, agility, social intelligence, and gratitude are the qualities one needs to adjust his or her shape to fit in the life puzzle. Those who are rigid find it harder to fit in.

I did not have a good time on weekdays. I looked forward to the weekends and spending time with Lucas. He was the only one who made me feel I had a life. Without my son, I felt empty.

Lucas liked to join me when I shaved. I loved when he put shaving cream on my face. Everywhere got messy and full of shaving cream. I did not mind it at all. It was the joy of life.

He liked *Andy's Prehistoric Adventures*. I bought three DVDs of the complete series for him. He often chose the episode, and I played it for him. His favourite one was the T-Rex and pumice stone. He was living in his imaginary Andy's world among dinosaurs. Sometimes, he asked me to become a T-Rex. I had so much fun with him.

He loved *Shrek* and *Toy Story*, especially Buzz Lightyear. His favourite movies were *Shrek 2* and *Toy Story 2*, which I watched a million times with him! When I was driving, he repeatedly asked, 'Are We There Yet?' like Donkey, and I had to say, 'Noooo,' like Shrek! He sometimes became an ogre.

In shopping centres, people asked his name, and he answered, 'I am Shrek. I am an ogre!'

I loved his playfulness.

On weekdays, I missed Lucas very much. Sometimes, I went to Emily's place to see him and play with him. Although Emily was welcoming, I felt no sense of belonging, like a stranger. She often prepared dinner and asked me to stay for dinner. However, I did not feel comfortable and left as early as possible.

Emily's place gave me a depressing feeling. It brought back the horrible memories of the shock she had given me when she'd left and took Lucas away from me at the start of his most intense phase of chemotherapy. I tried to change those destructive emotions with positive thinking, but I could not.

When I was at Emily's place, I usually stayed in Lucas's bedroom and played with him. Then we had dinner together like a family with some conversations between Emily and I, mostly about Lucas. Then I put Lucas to sleep and left.

I was still avoiding conversations with Emily because of all the negative feelings. I was still worried about saying something harmful.

When we had dinner, Emily pretended nothing had happened, which was annoying. I could not tell what was in her mind, but I could not trust her anymore.

I often thought about the possibility of reconciliation, but lack of trust killed the idea. I feared opening up the conversation with Emily.

What if I invest in re-establishing a life together and she dumps me? What if she takes the place I have bought from me and asks me to move out? What if she is only playing a game for financial reasons? Worries went through my head.

I often reminded myself about how kind and trustworthy Emily was, but I had mixed feelings and thoughts. I kept pushing myself to ask her if we could get back together, but it did not happen. I needed a strong desire for her, but it was not there. I could not trust her.

I had lost the feeling of love, and I doubted if I could find it again. It raised many questions in my head.

Have I ever loved her? I asked myself.

In an attempt to feel my love for her again, I looked at our pictures many times. I looked at the photos from when she was my girlfriend and the beautiful photos of our wedding ceremony. I noticed my big smile in those photos. However, it was annoying that I could not precisely remember my feeling of love for her.

I felt I was wounded, and I had to be careful not to allow her to hurt me more. I was still bleeding from the scar on my heart.

Not being with Lucas during the week was catastrophic for me. Lucas and I were missing out on our best years of father-and-son fun.

These feelings are temporary and will change. Only time will heal my sorrow. I hope I find love in my heart and the joy of life again. Stay strong and keep trying! I kept telling myself.

I thought about Lucas living with me, and I suggested to Emily that he could live with both of us fifty-fifty, but she did not accept. She believed he was too little and needed a mother more than a father. I did not insist, as I wanted to avoid an argument. I did not want us to be the type who would fight over our child and take our little boy to court. I would have opportunities later.

Emily was in contact with other mothers she had met in the oncology centre. In early December, she called me and said that two children with cancer could not survive. Jacob, with whom we'd shared a room for a week, had just died. I could not imagine what a trauma his lovely family would go through at Christmas.

The impact of those events on me was profound. I grew through emotional pain. I felt I knew people much better than before, and I could feel their emotions when they were around me. Something I had not been capable of before. It may sound unfamiliar to those who have not experienced it, but many people will relate to what I am saying here.

I had never felt emotional pain in my life until I saw my son in pain. No challenges in life could bring those experiences except parenthood and the unconditional love for my son.

I felt the pain and suffering others went through, and I learned how to listen and empathise with them. I pledged to myself that I would take any opportunity to offer my help and ease the pain of others by listening well with empathy. And if needed, I would share my experiences. Sometimes, just a few words of compassion and understanding might be the support one needs in tough times.

CHAPTER 9

Christmas

In December 2017, all of Sydney was full of beautiful sounds of Christmas and New Year. People were getting ready for the festive season, and shopping centres were full of families buying gifts for their loved ones.

I wandered in the shopping centres alone, wishing I had my lovely family to buy presents for each other. Well, I had my son, but I wanted a partner with whom to share love and affection. I was not feeling the joy of Christmas. I was sad and alone. I felt lost without my family.

My friends and colleagues told me about their holiday plans to enjoy their family time, but I had none of it. Sam had booked a villa for a week and asked if we would join. But with our deteriorated relationship, we could not.

I wanted to create a lovely Christmas for my son despite our separated family. When I was a kid, my dad gave me a ride-on car with manual pedals for my birthday. The wonderful memories of those exciting moments still bring a smile to my face. I wanted to buy a drive-on car for Lucas and spend time together during Christmas holidays to teach him how to drive the car.

I found a cool drive-on electric car online. It had features of a real car, like forward and reverse gears, an accelerator, music, a headlight, and even a reverse light. I could not find a similar one in shops.

When you're online shopping, the actual product may not be as good as the pictures shown on the website. But when I received and assembled the car, it exceeded my expectations. I was so excited to see Lucas driving his car. He would look super cute when driving it.

I bought a Christmas tree, decorations, a Santa train set going around the tree, and toys for Lucas. I told

Lucas stories of Santa giving him presents to prepare him for Christmas Eve. I wanted my son to have sweet memories of Christmas.

I could not wait until Christmas to see him driving his car, so I gave it to him earlier. On Saturday, 2 December, I put the car in my apartment and placed my mobile in a suitable position to record a video of his first reaction. The happiness and excitement in his eyes when he saw the car and jumped in it were priceless.

'It's not moving!' was the first thing Lucas said.

The car had a remote control for safety, which parents could use to control the car when needed. I moved the car using the remote control without him knowing. The surprise in his eyes, his joy, and the smile on his face were memorable. He then asked me to take him out to drive his car. In the first twenty minutes, he learned how to steer the wheel and use the accelerator pedal. He was feeling like an adult driving a real car. He was cutely serious when driving.

Christmas holidays started. I had time to take Lucas with me to shopping centres and take photos with Santa. He was excited about Santa and at the same time scared of the big furry man. Eventually, he stayed on Santa's knee by himself, and we took a cute picture.

I invited Emily to my place for Christmas Day to create a family time for Lucas. Christmas is all about family and children.

The Christmas tree decorations looked terrific, and Lucas loved it. On Christmas Eve when Lucas was asleep, I put little toys in a red Santa gift bag so that Lucas could unwrap his presents on Christmas morning. I then took a few pictures of the Christmas tree. I liked photography as a hobby, especially at night. Sometimes, I spent time adjusting the light and captured good photos. Emily never appreciated my passion for photography.

When Lucas woke up, I reminded him it was Christmas Day. He jumped out of his bed and ran into the living room, where he saw the red bag under the Christmas tree and excitedly shouted, 'Santa has brought me presents!'

His enjoyment when opening his presents made my eyes wet. I felt I had made my son happy after all he had been through.

Emily arrived later in the afternoon. We took family photos, and then we had dinner. Lucas was copying me in taking pictures. His style when he was trying to look like an adult photographer was so cute.

I created happy Christmas holidays for Lucas and made exciting moments for him. I felt I had not failed at being a father for my son, despite the challenges I had faced. I would always be there for him. I wished I could give him all that matters—to feel loved, beautiful, and wonderful.

Lucas liked it when we went to the waterside on the Sydney ferry wharves and sat there for a while. I felt he enjoyed spending time with his dad, doing nothing except sitting next to me watching water and ferries travelling. Sometimes, we hopped on a ferry, went to another wharf, and returned. He asked many questions, and I enjoyed explaining things to him.

I got a few games to play with Lucas, like Connect Four, building blocks, Lego, and a wooden train set. He loved playing Connect Four. He did not yet understand he had to get four of his checkers in a row, but I created a fun game that whoever dropped the last checker in a slot, would be the winner. He was so excited to drop the last one. He guffawed every time we both rushed to win. We played the game many times.

Lucas drove his car on weekends, and he was well known for his car in the neighbourhood. I also got him a scooter, which he loved and soon learned to ride it fast and furious. He was too fast for me. I had to run all the time, sweating and yet struggling to maintain the pace. I had to buy another scooter for myself to keep up with him. It was so much fun riding our scooters and exploring the mighty jungle in the Sydney Olympic Park with my lovely son. I felt much younger! Thank you, God, for those moments.

He always liked to sleep in my arms in my bed. He enjoyed playing with Mickey Mouse and Goofy dolls and a doll he got in the hospital; I named it Mr Button. I mimicked the voices of Mickey and Goofy and invented a funny voice for Mr Button, which he loved the most. He guffawed every time I played Mr Button.

I role-played with the dolls and told stories about being a caring boy. He listened well and repeated in his words the meaning I tried to get across. We often spent a good two hours playing in bed, and I told bedtime stories for him until he went to sleep. I then put him in his bed. I felt he resisted going to sleep early, not to miss the lovely moments with his dad.

Lucas enjoyed listening to me when I played guitar and sang. When I stopped, he asked me to continue. It reminded me of my father and how I had looked up to him when he sang for me—such beautiful and unforgettable father-and-son moments.

He also learned the name of the songs I played and asked me to play them. He liked me to play 'Greensleeves', 'Edelweiss', 'Twinkle', and 'Godfather'.

On Saturdays, I made pancakes for breakfast. Lucas enjoyed cracking the eggs and mixing the flour. We often clinked glasses and said 'cheers' when we drank tea, milk, or juice and drank a toast to everyone he liked—Mum; Dad; Mickey Mouse; Buzz Lightyear; Woody, and his imaginary characters, like El-She and Kaboo, who lived in Sydney corner, according to Lucas!

Lucas did not want to go back to his mum's place, because he missed me and had fun with his dad. Emily was kind to him, but he wanted his dad too. I felt it was confusing for him going back and forth between Emily and me. A little boy should not feel worried about losing his dad, and unfortunately, he was.

Returning him to Emily, leaving him, and saying goodbye was always hard for me, but I had to. His attempt to keep me staying longer was hurtful. Every single time, I had tears in my eyes while driving back to my loneliness. He often said to me, 'Daddy, don't go away. Okay?' or, 'I want you, Daddy.'

I wished my marriage had worked out well.

'When Mum comes to take me, you have to say, "No. Don't come," like that. You have to say, "Sorry, Emily. Lucas is too busy playing with me." And then you have to say, "Maybe go home and have some fun." And then you have to say, "Go away and let Lucas stay here",' said Lucas cutely while I was driving home after I picked him up from childcare.

These were his exact words I recorded on my phone. He was trying to convince me to let him live with me. I wished I could! I explained how much his mum loved him and assured him he would lose neither of us.

Some weekends, I baked an orange cake, and we went to a picnic in a nearby park. He had a favourite spot he liked us to sit and eat the cake.

Lucas enjoyed drawing and painting. I bought paints, coloured pencils and paper for him to have fun at his daddy's place. I spent time with him drawing funny characters and shapes. He enjoyed making paper characters, and sometimes he gave them to Emily as a gift.

I had thought Lucas was fond of riding our scooters and swimming. However, at childcare, his answer to the question favourite thing to do with Daddy was drawing. I did more of it after I realised that, and I noticed how much he enjoyed it.

While I was lonely and empty of love for a woman, I felt fulfilled when I was with Lucas. I enjoyed every second of my time with him. He was a gift in my life. I prayed for Lucas to be cured forever.

I knew the family was my life marrow, and I could see myself in gloom without my family. But my hurt feelings had paralysed me when it came to getting my family back together.

Many times, I convinced myself to ask Emily to work things out between us, with a hope of rebuilding our family. But when I saw her, I could not express it to her. I could not heal my pain and revive our broken trust and love. I was suffering from my solitude, but I could not make a relationship with Emily. I wished I could, which would be best for Lucas.

I hope 2018 will be a better year.

Printed in the United States
By Bookmasters